EXTREME SPORTS

RALLY CAR RACING

BY CHRIS BOWMAN

EPIC

BELLWETHER MEDIA • MINNEAPOLIS, MN

EPIC BOOKS are no ordinary books. They burst with intense action, high-speed heroics, and shadows of the unknown. Are you ready for an Epic adventure?

This edition first published in 2016 by Bellwether Media, Inc.

No part of this publication may be reproduced in whole or in part without written permission of the publisher. For information regarding permission, write to Bellwether Media, Inc., Attention: Permissions Department, 5357 Penn Avenue South, Minneapolis, MN 55419.

Library of Congress Cataloging-in-Publication Data

Bowman, Chris, 1990-
  Rally Car Racing / by Chris Bowman.
    pages cm. – (Epic: Extreme Sports)
  Includes bibliographical references and index.
  Summary: "Engaging images accompany information about rally car racing. The combination of high-interest subject matter and light text is intended for students in grades 2 through 7"– Provided by publisher.
  Audience: Grades: 2 through 7.
  ISBN 978-1-62617-352-1 (hardcover : alk. paper)
  1. Automobile rallies–Juvenile literature. 2. Rally cars–Juvenile literature. I. Title.
  GV1029.2.B685 2016
  796.7'3–dc23
                      2015030738

TABLE OF CONTENTS

WARNING

The drivers in this book are professionals. Rally car drivers always wear helmets and other safety gear when racing.

SPEEDING FOR GOLD

The green light flashes. Six rally cars take off. They push and bump each other around the first turn. The 2015 X Games rally car event is under way.

CROSS OVER
The X Games rally car racing event is called RallyCross.

The drivers battle for the lead. After five laps, Scott Speed gains first place. He holds off the other drivers for five more laps. Speed wins X Games gold!

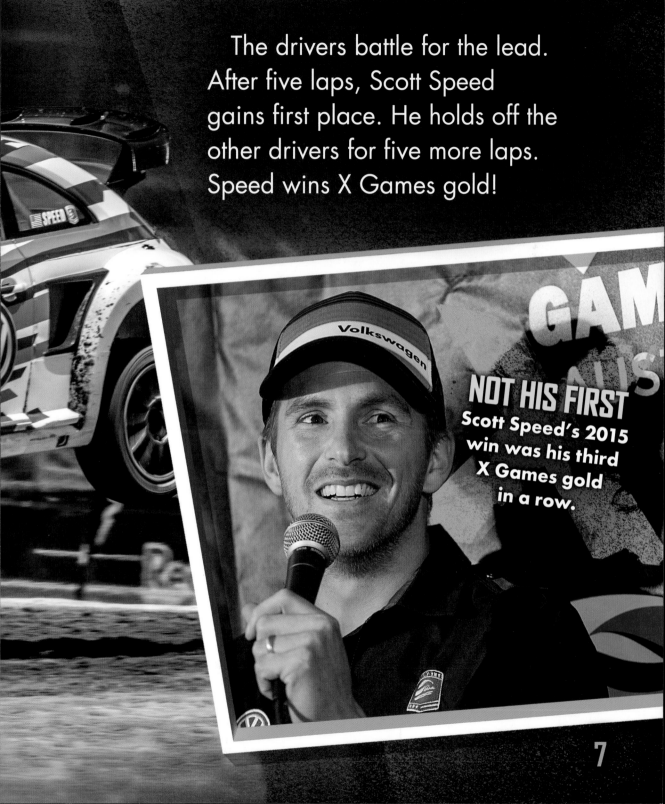

NOT HIS FIRST
Scott Speed's 2015 win was his third X Games gold in a row.

RALLY CAR RACING

Rally car races take place on **challenging** tracks. The cars speed around hairpin turns and fly over jumps. Navigators tell the drivers what is ahead on the road.

hairpin turn

PUT TO THE TEST
Rally drivers are not allowed to practice on the course at full speed before the race.

Races are held in all types of weather and on all kinds of road surfaces. Many events are on dirt trails through forests. They cover many miles and often last for days.

hairpin turns—tight, U-shaped turns

laps—complete runs around a track

navigator—a person who tells the driver what to expect on the road ahead; navigators are also called co-drivers.

rallycross—an event in which rally car drivers race at the same time around a track

stages—timed sections of a rally race

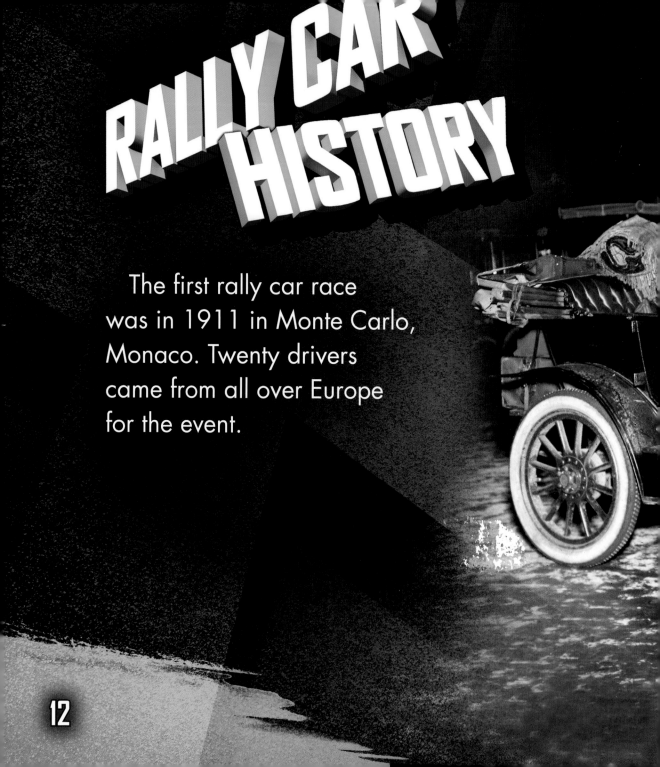

RALLY CAR HISTORY

The first rally car race was in 1911 in Monte Carlo, Monaco. Twenty drivers came from all over Europe for the event.

1911 Monte Carlo Rally

A WORLD SPORT

The first World Rally Championships were held in Monte Carlo in 1973.

By the 1960s, rally racing was very **competitive**. Today, rallies include drivers from all over the world. Rally racing is hugely popular in many different nations!

Rally in Ponta Delgada, Portugal

RALLY CAR GEAR

Rally car drivers wear helmets and neck braces. **Harnesses**, window nets, and **roll cages** also keep them safe during accidents. **Fire-resistant suits** protect drivers from burns.

roll cage →

USUAL SUSPECTS

The Ford Focus, Subaru WRX STI, and Volkswagen Golf are popular cars in rally racing.

Ford Focus

Subaru WRX STI

Volkswagen Golf

THE COMPETITION

Rally car races are **organized** into **classes**. Races usually have many stages. Each car races on its own. Its stage times are combined. Later, all drivers' times are compared. The driver with the fastest total time wins.

EVENT SCORING

In World Rally Championship races, the winner earns 25 points. Other top finishers also earn points. The driver with the most points at the end of a season wins the championship!

In rallycross, drivers race at the same time. These races are on closed tracks. The first driver to finish all the laps wins

INNOVATOR OF THE SPORT

name: **Colin McRae**
birthdate: **August 5, 1968**
hometown: **Lanark, Scotland**
innovations: **Became the youngest driver ever to win the World Rally Championship title in 1995**

GLOSSARY

challenging—difficult and requiring a lot of work

classes—different groups of races organized by engine size

competitive—wanting to be the best

fire-resistant suits—special clothes that drivers wear to protect themselves from burns

harnesses—straps and belts that keep rally car drivers in their seats

organized—planned ahead of time

roll cages—metal pipes inside rally cars that protect drivers in accidents

TO LEARN MORE

AT THE LIBRARY

Howell, Brian. *Rally Car Racing: Tearing It Up*. Minneapolis, Minn.: Lerner Publications, 2014.

Hurley, Michael. *Racing*. Chicago, Ill.: Raintree, 2013.

Sandler, Michael. *Rally Car Dudes*. New York, N.Y.: Bearport Pub., 2010.

ON THE WEB

Learning more about rally car racing is as easy as 1, 2, 3.

1. Go to www.factsurfer.com.

2. Enter "rally car racing" into the search box.

3. Click the "Surf" button and you will see a list of related web sites.

With factsurfer.com, finding more information is just a click away.

INDEX